Wallace & Gromit™
THE LOST SLIPPER
AND
THE CURSE OF THE RAMSBOTTOMS

Text by Tristan Davies

Drawings by Nick Newman

Hodder & Stoughton

Lettering by Gary Gilbert

First published in paperback in Great Britain in 1998
by Hodder & Stoughton
A division of Hodder Headline PLC

10 9 8 7 6 5 4 3 2 1

A CIP catalogue record for this title is available from the British Library

ISBN 0 340 69656 7

Printed by Jarrolds Book Printing, Norfolk

Hodder & Stoughton
A division of Hodder Headline PLC
338 Euston Road
London
NW1 3BH

DRAMATIS PERSONAE
(Which according to Gromit's written translation, is Latin for 'whom you are about to receive')

WALLACE
Inventor, handyman, cheese-fancier – and for the purposes of this story, a man who has lost his slipper but not his marbles.

GROMIT
Constant companion, housekeeper and dog – Gromit does all the doggy things you'd expect: he sits, he stays, he does algebra in his head while speed-knitting.

WILLIAM THE CONQUEROR
A conqueror from Normandy, called William, whose subjugation of the Anglo-Saxon people is a piece of cake compared to all the dreadful meals he is forced to eat in England.

BARON WALLAIS DE WALLAIS
Inventor, handyman and convicted coiffeur, this Norman ancestor was years ahead of his time when he tunnelled out of a French prison cell and under the Channel to England. Sadly, history only remembers him for his use of small furry animals with sharp teeth while trying to perfect a do-it-yourself medieval pudding basin haircutting system. It did not catch on.

UG-WALLACE
Inventor, handyman and non-shaver, this even more distant forebear held the world land speed rollerblading record (uncontested) in One Million Years B.C. A celebrated wit and conversationalist – if your idea of a good conversation involves going 'Ug-ug-ug' a lot.

WALLACE'S GREAT-GREAT-GREAT NEPHEW
Inventor, handyman and hopping mad eco-warrior, Great-Great-Great Uncle Wallace's future relative has a bee in his baseball cap about families who drive more than one pair of clogs.

THE PHARAOHS
Ancient Egyptians, sandal-wearers and confirmed cat-lovers, there's not much to say about Queen Neferti-tea-for-two-tu-tankha-etc. – except that it's much simpler just to call them Mr and Mrs Pharaoh.

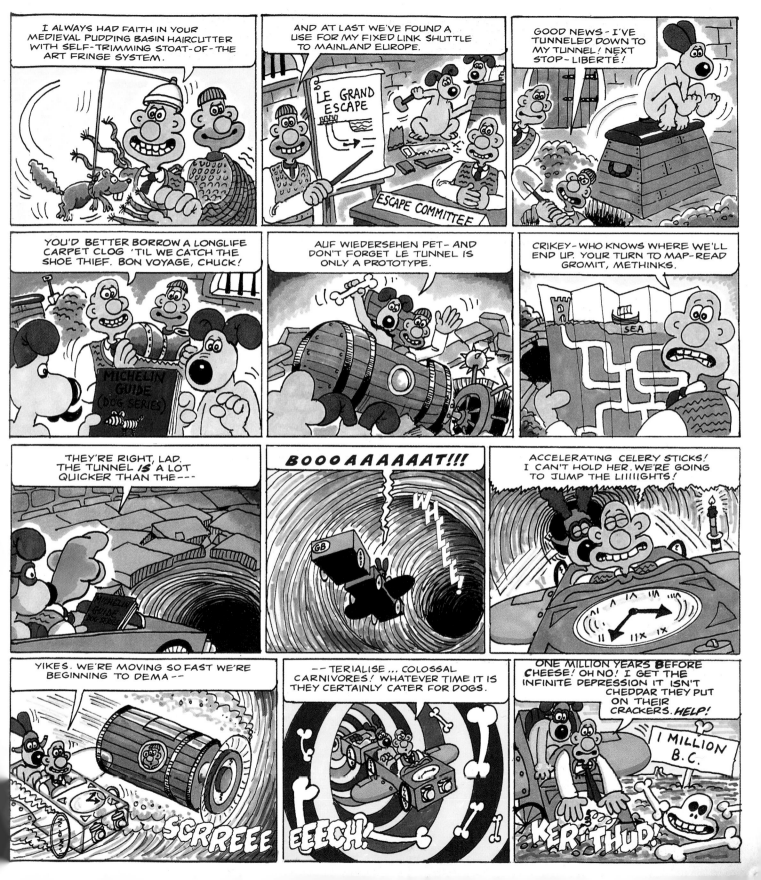

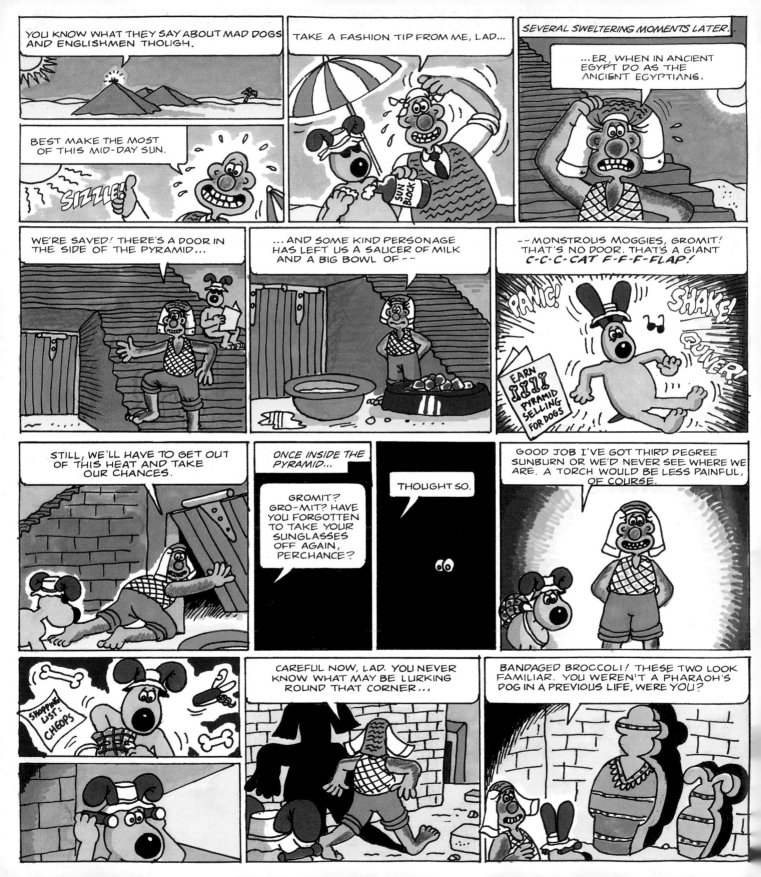

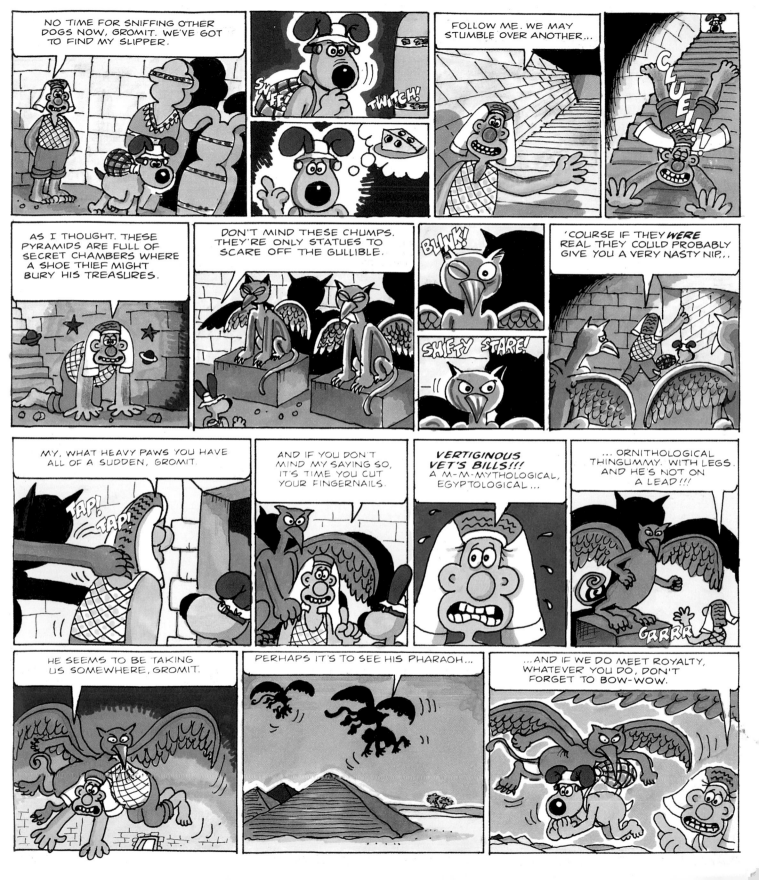

THE CURSE OF THE RAMSBOTTOMS

NIL DESPERANDUM, CHUCK!
(Which, along with *Per ardua ad Asda*, a traditional greeting at Roman supermarkets, is the only bit of Latin Wallace knows)

WALLACE
Inventor, handyman and gentleman motorcyclist, Wallace nurses a passion for the cheese of the Wensleydale region, and a tendresse for another local delicacy – the pulchritudinous Miss Wendolene Ramsbottom.

GROMIT
Bon viveur, bibliophile and barker, Wallace's constant travelling companion on the motorcycle is currently scripting a remake of Tennessee Williams' classic, *A Sidecar Named Desire*. Gromit's interest in bones remains undimmed, however. He is, after all, still a dog.

MISS WENDOLENE RAMSBOTTOM
Was there ever a maiden so fair as Wendolene, former wool shop proprietor and now the chatelaine of Ramsbottom Hall on 't' Ramsbottom Moor? Quite possibly there was – but not in this story there isn't.

PRESTON
Originally a cyber-dog created by Daddy, Wendolene's late father, Preston is undergoing modification as part of an ongoing series of improvements. Currently a cyber-butler powered by a rechargeable 12-volt car battery, everything is tickety-boo – except, that is, his voice control box which still suff. Ers. Tee. Thing. Probl. Ems. You get the pic. Ture.

RHETT LEICESTER
Charming, suave, debonair and sophisticated are just four of the flattering adjectives no-one in their right mind will ever apply to Rhett Leicester. An international cheese magnate, and Wendolene's lodger, Rhett's hobbies include garden gnomes and, er, garden gnomes.

BILL 'CHEESY' CHEESEMAN
* NOTE FROM THE PUBLISHERS: Due to circumstances beyond our control, no illustration is available of Mr Bill Cheeseman, Wensleydale's master cheesemaker. As you will read on the next page, he is currently missing on Ramsbottom Moor. We sincerely hope he turns up before the end of the story, and apologise for your temporary loss of picture.

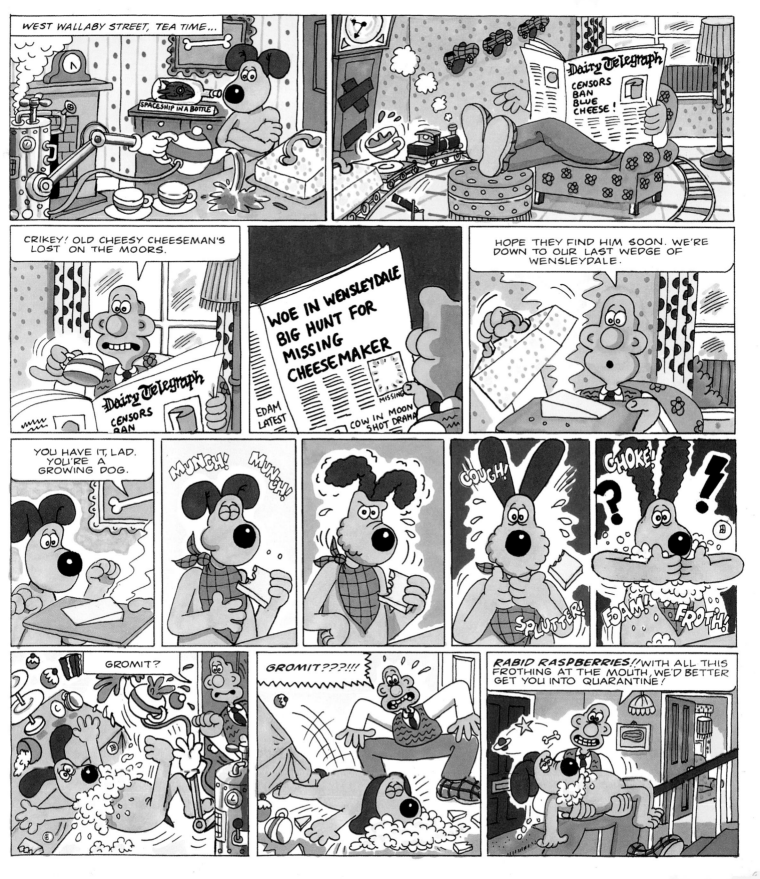

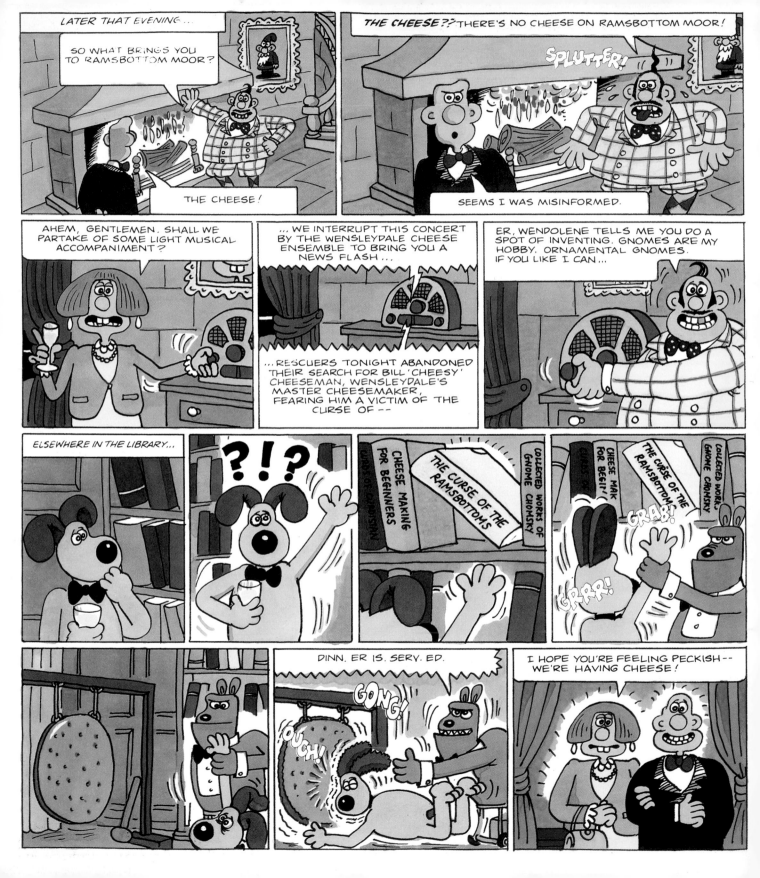

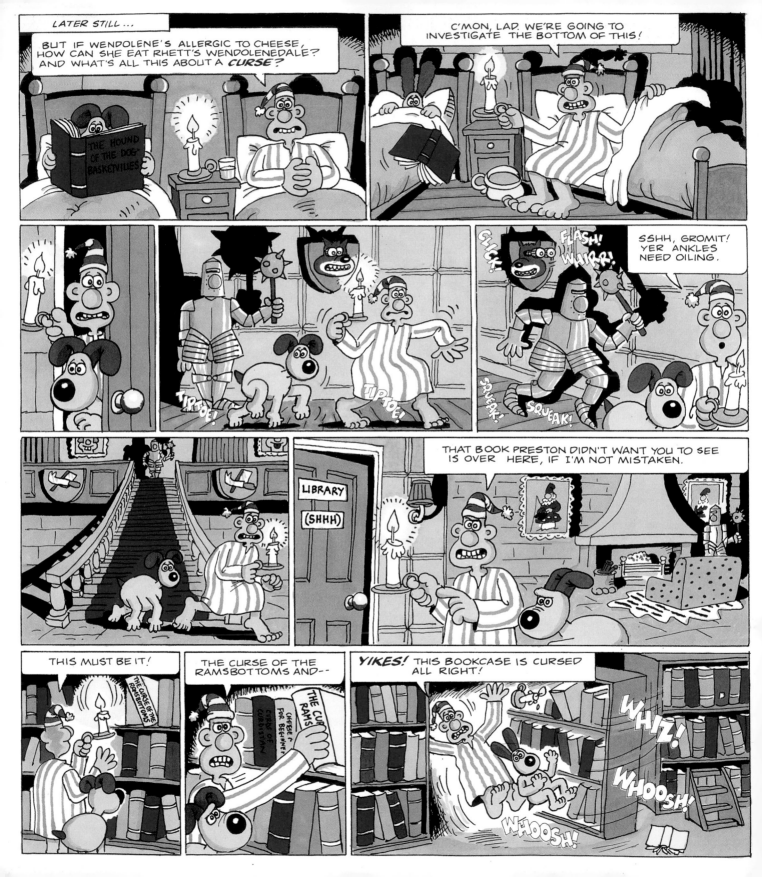

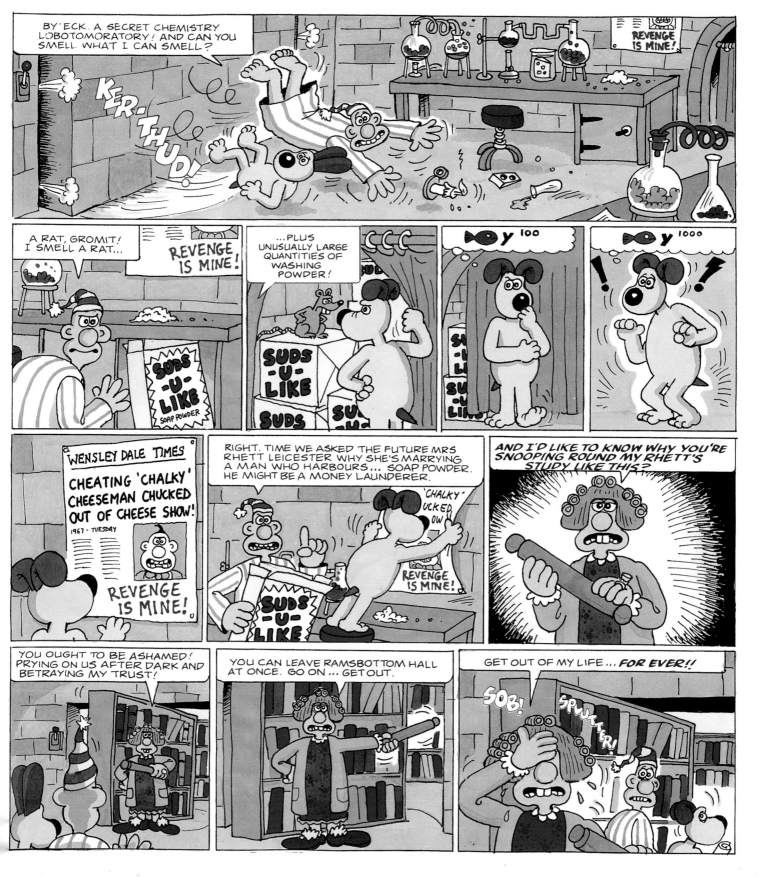

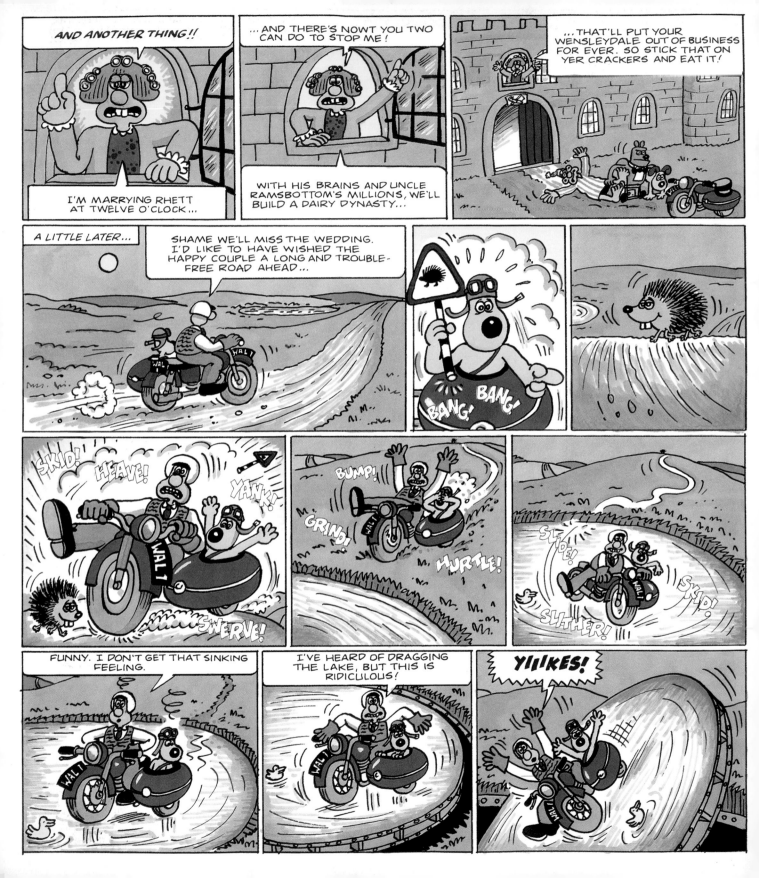

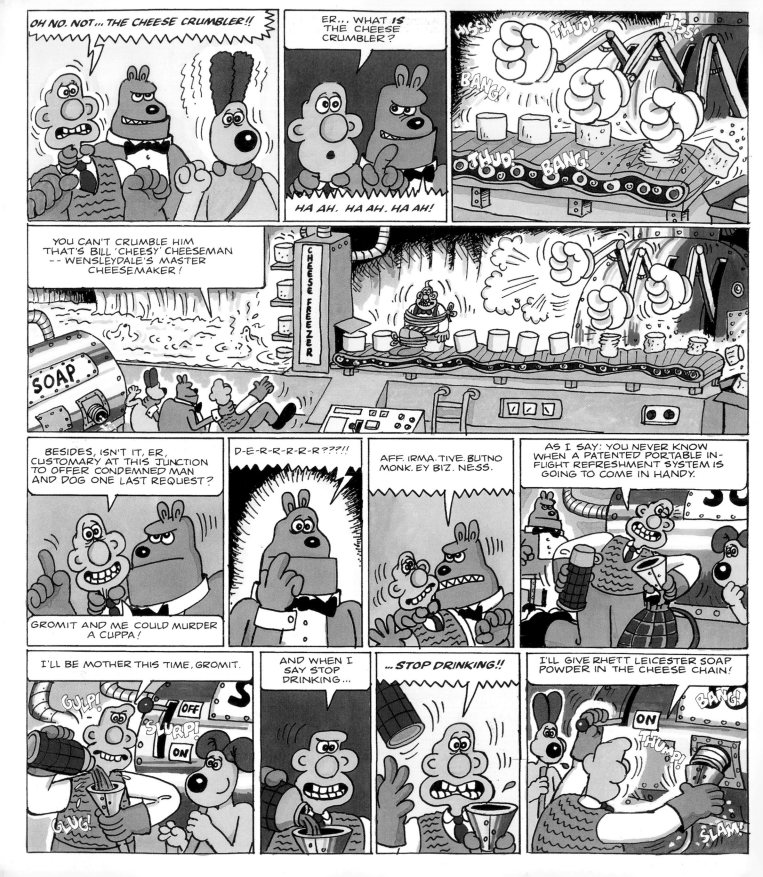

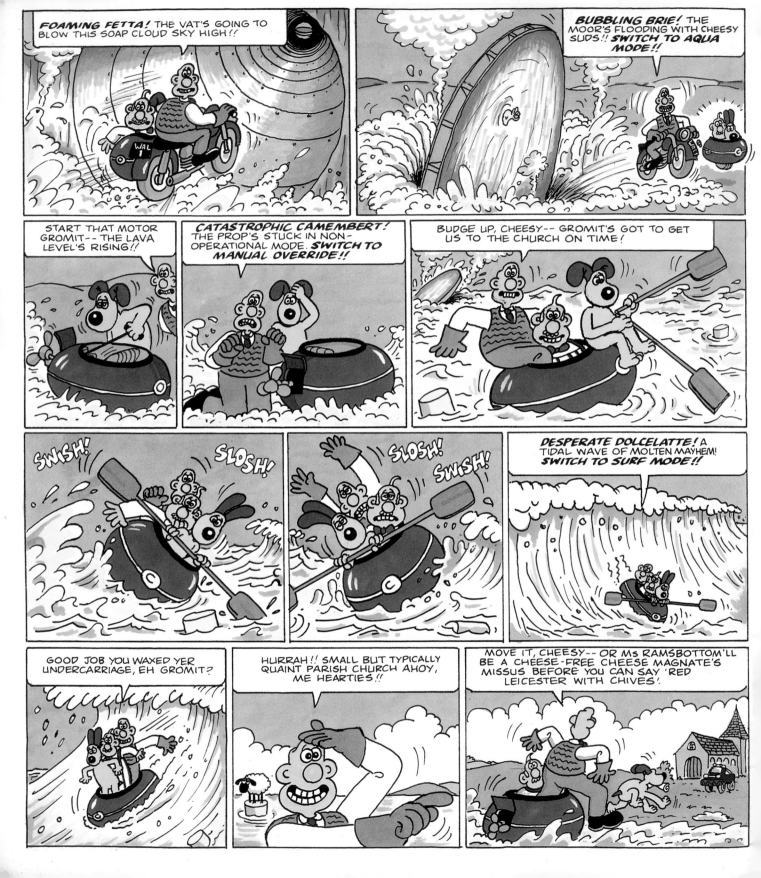

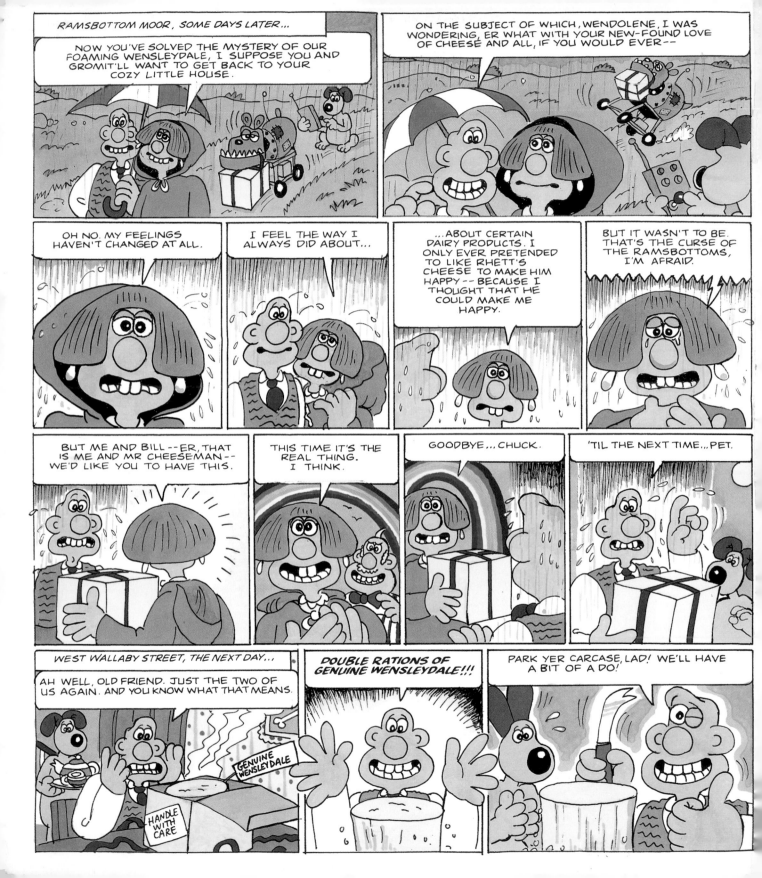